The Hawk Bandits
of Tarkoom

A Magical World Awaits You
Read

THE
SECRETS
OF
DROON

THE SECRETS OF DROON

The Hawk Bandits of Tarkoom

by Tony Abbott

Illustrated by Tim Jessell

A
LITTLE APPLE
PAPERBACK

SCHOLASTIC INC.
New York Toronto London Auckland Sydney
Mexico City New Delhi Hong Kong

Book design by Dawn Adelman

ISBN 0-439-20785-1

Text copyright © 2001 by Robert T. Abbott
All rights reserved. Published by Scholastic Inc.

SCHOLASTIC, APPLE PAPERBACKS, and associated logos
are trademarks and/or registered trademarks of Scholastic Inc.

12 11 10 9 8 7 6 5 4 3 2 1   1 2 3 4 5 6/0

Printed in the U.S.A.   40
First Scholastic printing, February 2001

For my brother Rick,
who knows that the adventure
doesn't have to end

Contents

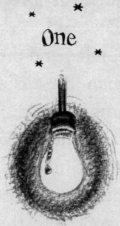

One

One Head Is Better Than Two

Eric Hinkle and his friend Julie carefully pulled open a small door under the stairs in his basement.

Errr-errrk! The door's old hinges squeaked.

Behind the door was a small, dark closet, with a single unlit lightbulb hanging from the ceiling.

"Isn't it weird how it looks just like a regular closet?" asked Julie.

Eric grinned. "It *is* a regular closet. To everyone else."

But to Eric, Julie, and their friend Neal, it was more than just a closet. It was the entrance to another world.

The magical world of Droon.

Actually, it was Julie who had first discovered the entrance to Droon.

She'd just gone into the closet, when suddenly the door closed behind her, the light went out, and — *whoosh!* — a long, shimmering staircase appeared where the floor had been.

The kids were scared, of course.

But the staircase looked so beautiful they just had to see what was at the bottom.

On their first visit to Droon, they met a young princess named Keeah who was now one of their best friends.

They'd also met a good wizard named

Galen Longbeard and his spider troll helper, Max.

Galen was teaching Keeah to be a wizard, too.

Together with Keeah and Galen, the kids had battled a wicked sorcerer named Lord Sparr, a strange witch called Demither, and lots of other nasty creatures who were always trying to take over Droon.

The best part was that Eric and his friends seemed to be helping Keeah keep Droon free.

"I asked you over," Eric said to Julie, "because I think we need to keep the closet in good working condition. After all, it's our only way into Droon."

"Great idea," said Julie. "If the door squeaks too much, your parents will hear us. And Galen told us always to keep Droon a secret."

"I'll put in a fresh lightbulb," said Eric.

"You can oil the hinges. I asked Neal to come and sweep up, but he's late."

"As usual!" Julie said with a laugh.

She took an oilcan from the workbench. Standing on her toes, she began oiling the door's hinges. Eric searched the nearby cabinets for a new lightbulb to replace the old one.

As they worked, Eric recalled their latest visits to Droon. He and his friends had had many adventures. But they'd also uncovered many mysteries.

For one thing, Keeah said she remembered being in the Upper World — Eric's world — a long time ago.

But that didn't seem possible.

Then, Keeah was told that Witch Demither secretly gave her some powers. Witch powers!

Keeah didn't remember that at all.

"Hey, Eric," said Julie, bending down to

oil the lower hinges, "what do you think witch powers are like?"

"I was just thinking about that!" said Eric.

"I mean, are they dark and dangerous like Lord Sparr's?" she asked. "Or more like the sort of natural wizard things Galen can do?"

"I don't know." Eric found a new light-bulb and took it to the closet. "But wouldn't it be weird if there was a connection between Keeah being here and having witch powers? I wonder if Galen knows."

"Galen's five hundred and forty-two years old!" said Julie. "If he doesn't know, who does?"

Eric shrugged. "Maybe we will. If we ever get to Droon again."

He glanced at a soccer ball sitting on the workbench. After their first visit to Droon, Keeah had put a spell on it. When the ball floated in the air, it meant the staircase would be open for them.

"I can't wait to go —" Eric began.

Just then, four furry white paws trotted past the window. They were followed by two beat-up sneakers.

"Get back here!" cried a familiar voice.

"Woof!" came the response.

"It's Neal," said Eric.

"And Snorky," added Julie. Then she laughed. "Looks like Neal's having trouble with him . . . again."

"We'd better help him out!" said Eric. The two kids dropped everything and rushed up the basement stairs, through the kitchen, and out to the backyard.

When they got there, Neal was on all fours, nose to nose with Snorky, trying to grab him.

Julie giggled. "It looks like you're dancing!"

"It's not funny," Neal groaned as Snorky romped away to sniff a tree. "I was teaching him to fetch when he escaped!"

Eric tried to trap Snorky from behind. "What was he fetching?"

"A box of cookies," Neal said.

Julie shook her head. "Only *you* would think of teaching a dog to fetch food for you."

Neal grinned. "What can I say? I'm a genius."

"Hey, genius, your dog just ran into my house!" said Eric. He jumped up the steps and into the kitchen.

Inside, Snorky skittered under the table and headed down the hall at top speed, tracking dirty paw prints the whole way.

"Not the living room!" said Eric. "My mom just vacuumed!"

"We'll trap him in the hall," Neal shouted, dashing through the kitchen.

Eric and Julie tore around the other way. But Eric slipped on the carpet, slid across the floor, and crashed down — *ka-thunk!* — taking Julie and a large house-plant with him.

The plant spilled dirt all over the carpet.

"Woof! Woof!" barked Snorky as he turned and shot down the stairs to the basement.

"Oh, no!" said Eric, scrambling to his feet. "What if Snorky gets into the closet?"

"Let's get down there right away!" said Julie.

But when they entered the basement, they stopped short.

Julie gasped softly. "Oh, my gosh!"

The soccer ball was floating in the air over the workbench.

"Keeah needs us in Droon," said Eric. "That means the stairs will be open for us."

"And for Snorky —" said Neal. "Uh-oh!"

The three friends spun around to see Snorky's curly tail disappear behind the closet door.

Click. The door closed softly.

"Yikes!" cried Neal. "He's going to Droon!"

"But he can't unless the light is out," said Eric.

He pulled open the door. The light *was* out.

"Oh, man! I didn't put the new bulb in!"

Below them, the stairs were shimmering in a rainbow of colors. And Snorky was prancing down them, his tail wagging happily.

"Come back here, you," said Julie.

The three friends dashed down the stairs, but Snorky began to run. *"Woof! Woof!"* he barked.

"He thinks it's a game!" moaned Neal.

As they descended through the clouds, the sky over Droon was turning from black to purple.

"It's just before morning," said Julie. "It should be getting light soon."

They jumped off the bottom of the staircase and looked around. Dusty brown mountains surrounded them on every side.

"It looks like the Panjibarrh hills," said Eric. "We've been here before. . . ."

"Never mind that," said Neal, scanning the rocky ground. "Where's Snorky? Snorky! Get back here. You need to go home —"

Then the staircase faded. The kids knew it would not reappear until it was time to go home.

"Too late to send Snorky back," said Julie.

Grrrr. Something was growling from behind a rock.

"Snorky?" said Eric cautiously. "Is that you?"

Grrrr! The growling was louder this time.

"Here, puppy," said Neal softly. "Here —"

A head peered from behind the rock.

But it wasn't Snorky's head.

It was large and gray. Its features were craggy and its skin was rough, as if it were very old.

Grrrr! Another head, the same as the first, jerked up from behind the rock.

"There are two of them!" said Eric, backing up. "Oh, man, we are cooked!"

The first head moved out from behind the rock and the second one moved with it. That's when they saw that both heads were on the same neck!

"That's definitely *not* Snorky," said Neal.

The beast growled, opening both sets of jaws. Four rows of huge fangs dripped a thick, yellow liquid.

Julie stepped back. "That is so — ewww!"

"Don't make it mad," Eric whispered.

GRR-RRR! The twin heads roared again.

"Too late for that," mumbled Neal.

The creature stomped toward them, then stood for a moment, roaring and growling.

Then it leaped at them.

Two

What the Legend Says

"Get down!" Eric cried, grabbing Julie and Neal. The three friends dove behind a large boulder just as the beast pounced.

Thoom! It shook the ground when it landed. Then it turned quickly.

"It's coming at us again!" said Julie.

Suddenly — *hrrrr!* — a six-legged, shaggy animal called a pilka thundered into the clearing.

"Stay back, you hideous thing!" cried a voice.

The kids looked up. Princess Keeah sat atop the pilka, her gold crown blazing in the dim light. She charged over the rocks at the beast.

"Keeah, watch out!" Eric shouted.

But Keeah rode forward, staring down the beast, her eyes blazing. "Begone!" she cried. "Or I'll . . . I'll . . . oh!"

Her left hand suddenly glowed with a sizzling red light. An instant later, a blast of red sparks knocked the two-headed creature back.

Eeeoow! Both heads howled angrily at her. Then, shrinking back, the beast clambered away through the rocks. In a moment, it was gone.

Just then, the great orange sun flickered over the mountaintops, and the purple sky brightened to pink. Morning had come to Droon.

"Wow, Keeah, that was awesome!" said Neal, jumping out from behind the boulder. "It was like that thing actually *obeyed* you!"

The princess slid down from the saddle and hugged her friends tightly. "I'm not sure why it did. But I'm glad it did! Are you all right?"

Eric breathed out in relief. "I think so. But in another second we would have been two-headed-dog food!"

"*Woof?*"

"Snorky!" Neal cried, whirling on his heels.

Trembling, the small dog stumbled toward the friends and leaped into Julie's arms.

"Poor Snorky," she said. "He's shaking."

"He's *my* pet, you know!" Neal grumbled. "I'm starting to think he doesn't really like me."

Keeah smiled. "Come on, everyone. I called you here because yesterday an earthquake rocked the Panjibarrh hills. King Batamogi found something strange and wants us to see. Galen's caravan is just ahead. Let's go meet him. We need to tell him about this beast!"

As the sun climbed over Panjibarrh's famous dust hills, the four friends rode Keeah's pilka down to the valley below.

Before long, they spotted two figures traveling across the plains.

"There's Galen!" said Julie. "And Max, too!"

Galen, his long white beard flowing above a blue cloak stitched all over with stars and moons, rode the head pilka. A tall cone-shaped wizard hat sat on his head.

Behind him rode Max, his spider troll helper. Max had eight furry legs, a pug nose, and wild orange hair. Two other pilkas were laden with supplies and saddlebags bulging with books.

"Hail, friends from the Upper World!" said Galen as the children rode up. "What news?"

"A two-headed beast attacked us!" said Eric.

Galen frowned. "Two-headed, you say?"

"And both heads were pretty ugly," said Neal.

The wizard stroked his beard as the children took turns describing the beast.

"It seemed old, yet it moved very quickly," said Keeah. "Luckily, I stopped it."

"Its four eyes were red and scary," Julie said.

"Also, it had fangs the size of bananas," said Eric. "Have you ever heard of such a thing?"

The wizard looked out over the hills. "I have," he said. "But what you say fills me with fear."

"Why?" asked Julie.

"Because," said Galen, "the beast you describe died four hundred years ago! Now, follow me. Quickly!"

With that, Galen snapped the reins of his pilka and tore ahead. The children stared at one another for a moment, then followed Galen into the hills. They didn't stop until they came to the place where a quake had split the ground wide open.

"So!" said Galen, staring at the jagged crack. "As I feared, this was no normal earthquake."

"Over here, my friends!" called a voice.

A furry creature with a whiskery snout and long, foxlike ears waved from atop a rock. He wore a green crown and a short green cape.

It was Batamogi, one of the ten kings who ruled the Oobja people of Panjibarrh. He jumped down from the rock and bowed first to Galen and Princess Keeah, then to Eric and his friends.

"A big rumbly-rumble shook the hills yesterday," Batamogi told them. "It sent me flying out of bed. I've been shaking ever since! This morning I found it. I called you here right away."

"Found *it*?" said Eric. "What did you find?"

Batamogi pointed to the deep gash in the earth. "An ancient tomb. See for yourselves!"

Galen dismounted his pilka and strode

over to the split in the ground. The wizard was very old, but he moved nimbly over the rocks and down into the ruined tomb.

At the bottom was a small square of earth. Pressed into the earth was the outline of a beast.

A beast that was not there.

A beast with two heads.

"Holy cow!" Julie gasped. "This must be the grave of the great-great-grandfather of that monster we saw."

"No, it *was* the monster you saw," said Galen, his eyes fixed on the outline. "This earthquake was no accident. It was ancient magic that opened the beast's tomb and set it free."

Keeah turned to Galen. "I thought it died a long time ago. Do you mean it didn't really die?"

The wizard did not answer. Instead, he

inspected every inch of the tomb. Finally, he climbed out and dusted his hands.

"The beast is called Kem," Galen said. "It was created by a magic as old as Droon itself. Long ago I fought the beast and buried it here, thinking it was dead. I was wrong, fooled by the dark magic. In his prime, Kem was watchdog of the old city of Tarkoom. He howled like a ghost before attacking intruders."

Eric and Neal shivered at the same time.

"Tarkoom?" squeaked Max. "That was a place of thieves! And robbers!"

"And terrible bandits!" said Batamogi, scratching his ears nervously. "But Tarkoom was destroyed ages ago. You can still see the ruins."

Galen pulled a thick scroll from his saddlebag. "True," he said solemnly. "I was there the night it fell. A great fire reduced the city to rubble."

"Good!" said Julie. "Serves it right."

Galen unrolled the scroll and read it. "Ah, but here lies the problem. A legend says that centuries may pass, but if ever Kem should howl again, Tarkoom would rise from its ashes."

"The city would just come back?" asked Neal.

Galen nodded. "And all the terrible creatures who lived there. Droon's old magic is powerful."

Keeah took a breath, looked at her friends, then back at Galen. "So, what do we do now?"

"We wait in the hills above the Panjibarrh Valley," said the wizard, rolling up his scroll again. "If Tarkoom does rise again, we'll have a most important job ahead of us. Until then, we wait and watch."

Eric frowned. "What exactly will we see?"

"The past," said Galen. "We will see the dark past of Droon coming back!"

Three

Tarkoom . . . Again!

For the next hour, Batamogi led the small troop up one dusty path and down another. They were heading for the highest point in all the Panjibarrh hills.

"Who lived in Tarkoom?" Julie asked.

"Hawk bandits, they were called," Galen said, fixing his eyes on the road ahead. "Half human, half bird. As terrifying to see as they were ruthless. But worst of all was their leader, Ving."

Batamogi nodded, shivering. "The stories say he possessed a strange, soothing voice. It made his victims feel safe. Then he swooped down on heavy wings — *fwit! fwit!* — and robbed them of everything! Oh, Ving and his bandits were feared across all of Droon."

"Until my master stopped them!" said Max, beaming proudly.

"Four hundred years ago," said Galen, his pale cheeks blushing. "But now we must do it again. You see, Tarkoom was a city in the ancient empire of Goll, an evil realm of dark magic from Droon's earliest times. After a long struggle, Goll — like Tarkoom itself — was destroyed."

"But its magic still lives!" Max added.

Galen nodded. "Indeed it does. If Ving and his bandits come to life and work their evil on present-day Droon, I fear the whole dark past of Goll may live again. If I am right, we must stop Ving from changing our world in any way —"

The earth trembled suddenly.

"Another rumbly-rumble!" said Batamogi as Snorky jumped into his arms.

Galen stopped his pilka on a ridge and looked down. "And here we are!"

Below them lay the vast Panjibarrh Valley.

In it were piles of rock, crumbled stones, broken columns, sunken streets, and collapsed buildings.

"Tarkoom," said Batamogi under his breath.

"That's the place?" said Neal, looking down at the ruined city. "Doesn't look too lively."

The earth trembled beneath their feet again.

"Just wait . . ." the wizard said. "Even

now, Tarkoom prepares to return. Let us make camp."

The eight adventurers made a small encampment in a clearing overlooking the ruined city.

Galen sat on a boulder with his scroll and took up the watch.

Max watered the pilkas, while Keeah unpacked some snacks and passed them out.

"Food, anyone?" she asked.

"*Woof!*" barked Snorky.

"It figures!" said Neal, shaking his head. "'Food' is the only word he understands."

"Oh, is that so?" said Batamogi, turning to Snorky and scruffing him. "Well, let's just see!"

The Oobja king let Snorky sniff the cuff of his sleeve. "Now, Snorky, stay here. . . ."

Batamogi backed up slowly, then scurried off behind some big boulders. A moment later, he called out, "Snorky . . . fetch!"

In a flash, Snorky bounded up and, sniffing along the ground, trotted away into the rocks.

A moment later Batamogi waddled back to the camp with Snorky nipping at his heels. "Ho-ho!"

"That was awesome!" said Neal. "Snorky, now me!" He went and hid himself among the rocks. "Snorky . . . fetch!"

The dog went over to Max, curled up, yawned, and fell asleep. Then he began to snore.

"Poor Neal!" said Keeah when Neal returned glumly. "I'm sure Snorky likes you very much, in his own way."

Hours went by. The day wore on into evening. And still Galen read the scroll, kept watch, and said nothing.

"It's getting cool," said Keeah. "I wish we had . . ." All of a sudden — *fwoosh!* — a small fire appeared before them, its flames crackling. The princess jumped back.

"Where did that come from?" she said.

For the first time in hours, Galen moved, looking over at the princess. "You did that, Keeah," he said. "It is one of your *other* powers."

Eric shot a look at Julie. They both remembered what they had spoken about earlier that day. That Keeah had . . . *witch* powers.

"We may never know how you got these powers," said Galen, "but you must learn to control them."

Keeah frowned. "I'm sorry. They seem to come from nowhere and just . . . happen."

"Like when you helped your mother

change from a tiger to a dolphin?" asked Julie, remembering their last adventure in Droon.

"Or when you scared Kem away," said Neal.

Keeah nodded. "It frightens me a little. Well, a lot. The magic seems very strong. And wild. I'm afraid I might hurt someone."

"Pah! Never!" said Max firmly. "You are a very fine young wizard. And I don't believe you were ever alone with any witches. Besides, your father says it's impossible —"

"That mystery must wait, Keeah," Galen said, standing quickly. "Tarkoom . . . begins to wake!"

As the last streaks of sunlight cut across the ruined stones, the valley rumbled even more.

Once. Twice. A third time.

The piles of old rubble and broken stones shivered and shook and rocked and rattled.

Finally — *ka-phooom!* — the ground quaked from one end of the valley to the other.

And it happened.

The toppled stones of the wrecked city of Tarkoom seemed to fly up one by one and set themselves neatly back into place.

Columns, walls, towers, gardens!

Stone by stone, Tarkoom was rebuilding itself from its own ruins!

"Oh, my gosh," Julie exclaimed. "It's coming back. Tarkoom is coming back!"

Four

City of Bandits

As they all watched, the centuries-old city of Tarkoom shuddered slowly into the present.

Where rocks had lain scattered on the plain, now great buildings stood.

Dusty piles of tumbled stones were now the sturdy towers and turrets of a monumental city.

Tarkoom was back, glowing within high walls of red- and honey-colored stone.

And at its center stood a giant domed palace.

"It's beautiful," said Keeah under her breath.

"Beautiful, perhaps," said Galen. "But full of bandits who will try to stop us from doing what we must do."

"So," said Neal, "*their* mission will be to stop *our* mission. But what exactly *is* our mission?"

The wizard let a smile crease his lips as he tapped his scroll. "My friends, we must do nothing less than destroy Tarkoom!"

"The whole city?" asked Eric. "But how?"

"We must somehow use Ving's own plan against him," the wizard replied. "The legend is most specific about this. If I am right, he will mount an attack tonight. If he succeeds, he will have altered Droon in our time. He and his bandits will have become part of it."

"Oh, dear!" said Batamogi. "An attack! I hope not on my poor people!"

"But we'll stop him," said Keeah firmly.

"Only if we hurry!" said Galen.

Leaving their pilkas at the camp, the band of eight travelers climbed down into the valley.

For most of the way, the only sound was their own careful plodding through mountain passes. And the sound of Snorky whimpering.

At last, the narrow way opened up to an awesome sight. Galen held up his hand.

"The entrance to Tarkoom!" he declared.

Hewn from the face of a cliff was a large arched opening. It soared up from the ground as high as two houses. Its sides were cut into the red stone and glowed crimson in the moonlight.

"Awesome," said Eric. "But scary. Look."

Above the opening, a giant hawk head was carved into the cliff wall.

Its eyes were shimmering jewels that seemed to stare down on anyone who might enter.

"That is the image of Ving, leader of the bandits," said Galen. "He loves only himself."

"No kidding," Neal mumbled. "It's like having a picture of yourself on your front door!"

"Let us enter," said Galen softly.

The moment he set foot through the arch — *eeoow!* — the howling of the two-headed beast rose up from deep within the city streets.

"Kem is doing his job," Keeah said with a shiver. "He really is the city's watchdog."

"Which means the bandits will soon know we're here," said Julie. "Be careful, everyone."

They passed into a street lined by columns of polished red stone. The buildings on either side were carved deep into the valley cliffs.

The black holes of their doors and windows were like eerie eyes staring out of the past.

"Everything looks so new," said Keeah. "It almost feels as if we're going back in time."

Galen shook his head. "No, Tarkoom has invaded the present. At this very moment, Ving sits in his palace, hatching his terrible plot to stay in our world."

"And staying in our world," said Batamogi, "means the dark past of Droon will come again!"

"That's why we need to destroy the city!" Max chirped. "So the past will leave the present and go back to the past so our present will be safe for the future!"

Neal blinked. "Will there be a quiz on this? Because I'm getting a major headache."

Eric tried to laugh, but he couldn't. He didn't quite understand it, either.

He paused to sort it out in his head.

"Okay," he mumbled, counting on his fingers. "One, Tarkoom is a city from the past, right? But, two, the earthquake sort of released it from the past, and now, three, it's in the present. Okay, it's some magic thing that only happens in Droon. Now we need to — four — find out what Ving is up to and — five — stop him. Then, six, we wreck the city so it goes back to the past where it belongs. Neal, is that right? Does that make sense to you? Neal?"

Eric looked up from his hands. He was alone.

The others had turned a corner and were already heading toward the palace.

"Hey, guys, wait up!" Eric called out. "Guys!"

Thump.

He stopped. He suddenly felt icy cold.

To his right, he glimpsed something in one of those open windows. Red eyes — four of them — flashing in the darkness.

"K-K-Kem?" Eric whispered. "Oh, no. It's Two-head! It's him! It's it! It's . . . oh, help!"

Eric tore off down the street, but somehow — *thump! thump!* — Kem leaped down in front of him, both heads growling.

Then it reared up and jumped at him.

Eric shot around the corner, but his friends weren't there. He must have taken a wrong turn!

Eeoow! Kem howled and thomped even faster after him. Eric dashed around another corner.

Suddenly, he found himself inside a walled garden. It was thick with hanging plants and vines creeping up the walls.

Kem bounded right in after him.

Eric tried to scream, but no sound came out.

Kem slowed, growling under its breath. Step by step it came closer.

Eric looked around. There were hard-shelled fruits about the size of softballs growing on the vines. He tugged one off and threw it at Kem.

Crack! The fruit clattered and broke on the ground. *Plooff!* It gave off a horrible stink.

"Oh, phew!" Eric gasped, staggering back.

The fruit smelled like something rotten. Worse than garbage. *Worse* than worse than garbage!

But Kem kept coming, closer and closer.

With his last ounce of strength, Eric clutched the hanging vines and pulled himself up the wall, tossing more stinky fruits the whole way.

Crack-crack! Plooff!

"Get away, you — thing!" Eric cried.

Then — *krrippp!* — the vines tore away from the wall. Eric slammed to the stony ground.

Kem leaped at him, but the ground gave way and Eric fell *through* it. Down, down, down he went — straight into the open earth.

Five

The Everywhere Passages

Eric slid, rolled, tumbled, then slid some more until — *thwump!* — he hit the bottom.

"Oww!" he groaned. Every part of him ached.

He gazed about, but it was too dark to see. He felt on every side with his hands. There was hard, packed dirt all around.

"I'm in some kind of pit," he mumbled.

Looking up, he saw a glimmer of

moonlight far away at the top. Very far away.

"Neal! Julie! Keeah!" he cried out.

No answer. Not even the howling and growling of Kem. Eric twisted until he got to his feet. It was hard because the hole was so narrow.

"Galen! Keeah! Help!" he yelled up.

Still, no answer.

Reaching with both arms, he tried to climb, but the sides of the pit were smooth and steep. The more he tried, the faster he slid back down.

"Oh, come on!" he cried. "People! I'm down in this pit! Come and get me —"

"*Spluff . . . muffle . . . pluggh . . . wuff!*"

Eric froze. "Wh-wh-who's there?"

"*Muffle . . . wuggh?*" was the response.

Something was in the pit with him!

Two somethings.

Their noises sounded like words, but of

course they weren't. Then they started scratching.

"They're just digging," Eric said, breathing out slowly. "They won't bother me. They'd better not!"

After a while the sounds died down.

Eric yelled for what seemed like hours.

Why wouldn't they answer? Were they searching Tarkoom for him? What was going on?

Over and over, Eric yelled out his friends' names. His voice became hoarse. His throat hurt.

Finally, he gave up. He hunched up in a ball, tired and achy all over. Exhausted, he fell asleep.

When he woke up, light was streaking across his face. He looked around. Then he looked up.

Droon's sun crossed over the mouth of the pit.

"Holy crow!" he cried. "I've been here all night? Oh, man! Neal! Julie! Keeah! Get me out!"

Still, there was no answer.

Eric felt a sharp pain in his stomach. Hunger.

Of course he was hungry! It had been a day since he'd eaten. His stomach was empty.

Looking up, he tried once more to climb out, but this time he felt something round and hard under his foot.

He reached down and grabbed it.

"Yuck!" he said.

It was one of those smelly fruits he'd found in the garden. Luckily, this one was still in its hard shell. It must have fallen into the pit with him.

He was ready to toss it, when he had an idea.

"The shell is hard and curved," he said

to himself. "If I crack it open, maybe I can use the shell to dig my way out!"

"Sp-p-pluff . . . m-muffle!"

Eric laughed. "Prepare to be grossed out, little guys." He took a deep breath, then slammed the shell as hard as he could on the ground.

Crack! The shell split open.

Whoosh! The smell poofed out. It seemed to hit his face directly, like a fist.

"Akkkk!" Eric groaned. In the cramped space, the smell seemed even worse than before.

"Spliiiifff!" the creatures cried.

"I agree!" said Eric, pinching his nose tight.

He picked up the broken shell. The fruit inside was dark pink and juicy. He needed to clear it out to use the shell to dig.

He began to pry out the fruit with his fingers.

His stomach ached again suddenly. The hunger was back.

"No way!" he cried. "I'm not going to eat it!"

But he couldn't stop himself.

Slowly, Eric placed a small bit of the fruit in his mouth. Its cool juice swam on his tongue. Holding his breath, he swallowed. Then he breathed again.

He gasped. "What . . ."

The fruit tasted sweet! It was delicious!

"Raspberries!" he said aloud. "That's it. Raspberries, with sugar on top!"

Eric devoured the entire fruit in seconds.

Then he slurped up the extra juice left in the shell. Then he licked every drop from his fingers.

The most amazing thing was that when he breathed again, he no longer smelled the terrible odor of the pod. All he tasted was the wonderful flavor on his tongue.

"This is the most delicious food I've ever eaten!" he cried. "I've never tasted anything so —"

"Please keep it down," whispered a voice.

Eric froze. "W-w-w-what? Who's there?" he stammered.

"You're talking too much," said another voice.

Two pairs of eyes blinked at him from the shadows. They moved into the dim light.

"Whoa!" Eric gasped.

The creatures looked a little like otters. Sleek brown hides covered their short, slender bodies. Their heads were crowned by bright tufts of spiky white fur.

Their eyes were large and round and friendly.

"You're t-t-talking!" Eric said.

"Of course," answered the first. "It's how we communicate. You seem to have learned it, too!"

"But how can I understand you?" Eric asked.

"The tangfruit," said the second. "Its taste is magic. By eating it, you can understand us."

"And in case you couldn't tell," said the first, "you are now speaking our language. The effect will wear off, of course. It always does. By the way, we are called mooples. We live here."

"Pleased to meet you," said Eric. Then a question suddenly exploded in his head. "Wait. If you live here, you must know a way out!"

"A way out of the passages?" said the second. He began to chuckle and snort.

"Where do you want to go? The passages can take you everywhere!"

Eric's heart leaped. "Up there!" He pointed to the top of the pit.

"Just follow us," said the first moople. "Of course, the way in is never the way out. The passages wind and wind. And . . . here we go!"

The two creatures took Eric through a vast maze of holes. Tunnels upon tunnels. Passages leading to other passages, weaving up and around, crisscrossing each other like a pretzel.

"The passages weave throughout all of Droon," said the first. "Under mountains . . ."

"Under castles," said the other. "Volcanoes."

"Underwater?" said Eric as they crawled by a bubbling pool. "Does that lead to the ocean?"

He wondered if the tunnels led to the dark lands of sorcerers . . . and witches.

"The passages lead everywhere!" said the first.

"And they go on forever," said the second.

"They are all over Droon. You may fall in them again sometime," said the first moople.

"And be welcome, too!" added the second.

"As *she* was, poor pretty thing," said the first.

Eric stopped. "There was someone else here?"

"A child. A girl," said the second. "She had such nice manners. Poor thing was lost, I think."

"A girl was lost in the passages?" said Eric.

The first moople scrabbled up through

the dirt. "We tried to help her. Then —
poof! — a big light, and she was gone.
Years ago that was."

The other began to snort again. "Years
ago! That's funny — if you know what I
mean!"

Eric blinked. "Not exactly —"

"You will!" said the first. "And here you
are!" He pointed to an opening above
them. Fresh air poured in. And moonlight.
It was night again.

"Now we must say good-bye," said the
first.

"'Bye. And thank you!" said Eric.

"You are welcome anytime!" said the
other.

The mooples scurried away into the
darkness.

"Strange creatures," Eric muttered. "But
nice."

His arms hurt, his head ached, he was

exhausted, but the smell of fresh air drove him up.

Finally, he slid through the opening. Moonbeams lit an empty street of red cobblestones. Kem was nowhere to be seen.

"Of course not," Eric said to himself. "That was, like, two days ago!"

Eric could hardly believe that after all that time and after all that traveling he was only a few paces away from where he'd started. "Amazing," he mumbled.

He spotted the Tarkoom gate in the distance and went straight for it. Then he heard voices.

He darted into the shadows and peered out.

"He was just here, wasn't he?" said one voice.

"Yeah," said another. "Then he was gone . . ."

Eric's mouth dropped open. It was

Julie and Keeah! And Max and Neal and Batamogi!

"Oh, my gosh!" gasped Eric, staggering over to them. "Guys! Guys! I'm here. You found me!"

"Where did you go?" asked Julie. "We couldn't see you for a minute."

Eric blinked. "For a minute? I was stuck in that pit forever! Then I ate the stinky fruit and now it's tomorrow and — I yelled so much! Why didn't you answer?"

Batamogi and Max looked at each other.

"Eric, you were gone for, like, thirty seconds, tops," said Neal. "What's the big deal?"

"Thirty seconds! It was two days!" Eric said.

Keeah frowned. "No, wait. Something is strange about this. Eric, tell us what you saw."

He told them everything that had happened to him. The creatures he had met. What they told him about the passages. How he wasn't the first one from above to have been there.

"Very strange," said the princess. "I think I've heard about these passages somewhere. Magical tunnels that wind around and around until you get lost in them. And what seems like days there takes no time here."

"Perhaps my master has heard of these passages," said Max. "I wonder if they can help us in our mission to stop Ving."

"Good idea," said Julie. "We'd better catch up to Galen. He went on ahead to find a way into the palace —"

"You there!" snarled a strange voice. "Stop!"

Suddenly — *fwit! fwit!* — the sound of heavy wings filled the air around them.

"Hawk bandits!" cried Batamogi. "Flee! Flee!"

But it was no use. In seconds, all seven travelers were surrounded by an ugly band of bird-headed creatures. They grabbed them with sharp claws and pushed them roughly down the street.

"Bring them to Ving!" one bandit cried, clacking his greasy beak. "He'll be very angry!"

Six

In the Court of Prince Ving

"Let us go!" Keeah cried, trying to get free.

But the bandits only gripped her and the others tighter, dragging them down one cobbled street after another until they reached the palace.

"I hope Galen's okay," Julie whispered to Neal.

Neal nodded. "Maybe he can save us —"

"Silence!" snapped a bandit with a large

stomach and broken wing feathers. He glared at Eric. "You! Tell me where the wizard is."

Before Eric could answer, Max snarled, "We don't know! And we wouldn't tell you if we did!"

"Nice crown you got there!" said a skinny bandit who looked as if he wanted to peck Batamogi to pieces. "Ving will like that!"

"And I like that little morsel!" said the broken-wing bandit, casting his eyes on Snorky, who was shivering in Max's arms.

The kids were pushed from a dark hallway into a huge chamber. In its center stood a colossal stone statue towering up to the high ceiling.

It was a statue of a man with a bird head.

"Ving," snarled Keeah, guessing who it was. "Galen said he loves himself. This proves it."

In the flickering light of a dozen burning torches sat the bandit prince. Ving had a large green bird head and an orange beak that curved down angrily at the tip. Two black eyes the size of baseballs bulged on either side of his face.

From the chest down, except for his feathery arms and his sharp claws, Ving was like a man. He wore armor that was deeply gashed and nicked from many battles.

"Icthos!" Ving called, and the bandit with the broken wing thumped across the floor to him.

Eric tried to hear what they were saying.

"Where is the old wizard?" Ving whispered.

"We did not find him," the bandit told him.

Eric glanced around at the huge room.

He wondered how close Galen was. Was he already planning to rescue them? Had he discovered Ving's plans?

The hawk prince sat up. "Release these people! They are our guests, and free to go!"

"Free to go?" said Keeah as the bandits unhanded her and the others. "But you and your men are thieves and robbers of the worst kind!"

Ving hung his head and sighed, his wings rustling. "That was true once, my dear. But now Tarkoom has risen from its ashes. And we have been given a second chance!"

The words sounded soothing, like a bird cooing softly. Eric felt that Ving might not be as bad as they thought. He *did* say they could go.

"We come back to Droon not to steal again," Ving said softly, almost warbling.

"We welcome this chance to live in peace with all Droonians!"

. . . And rob Droon's most precious treasure!

Eric nearly jumped when he heard those words. What? What! He looked around. None of the others seemed to have heard Ving say that.

Ving turned to Batamogi, Max, and Snorky. "Icthos, take your men, and show the Oobja king, the spider troll, and the dog to my room so that they may refresh themselves."

. . . Put them to work down below!

Eric gasped. He glanced at the others.

Again, no one had heard the words!

In fact, Batamogi was smiling.

"Thank you, Prince Ving," the Oobja king said. "Perhaps we were mistaken about you. You are welcome in our village anytime!"

Eric couldn't believe his ears. "Wait —" he began, but already the three friends had been whisked from the room.

Ving spoke again in the same soothing tone. "Now, while we await your wizard friend," he said, "how would you like some food?"

Neal slapped his hands together and smiled. "Now, that's more like it. I am so starving!"

"Me, too," said Julie. "And a chance to wash up would be great, too."

. . . Oh, you'll be washed up, all right!

Eric couldn't be quiet any longer. He nudged Princess Keeah. "What's going on here? Don't you hear what he's saying?"

But even Keeah was smiling as Ving went on speaking about the feast he would give them.

. . . Get that wizard once and for all . . . raid everyone's treasures . . . and terrorize

Droon as we did four centuries ago! Oh, the past shall live!

Eric listened carefully to the words. It was plain that he was hearing more than the others were hearing. But how could he? Why him?

Then he understood.

"The tangfruit!" he said to himself. In the same way he had heard the furry mooples in the passages, now he understood what Ving was *really* saying. Eric was hearing the truth! The truth behind the lies! And it was all because of the tangfruit!

Keeah stepped forward. "Thank you, Ving. A celebration sounds wonderful. You are kinder than we thought you might be."

Of course! thought Eric. Even Galen had said that Ving had magic in his voice.

Ving bowed his feathery head and

cooed some more. "I am often misunderstood, I'm afraid."

. . . It is you who will be afraid. . . .

Ving then began to speak to his pirates in a language of clacks and grunts and whistles.

Prepare the bolt. Once these children and their wizard have been taken care of, we will fire the bolt. Then we shall be part of Droon's present. And its greatest treasure shall be ours! Go!

Eric's blood ran cold as some bandits bowed, then fluttered out of the chamber.

It will be our biggest theft, he heard them say.

Turning once more to the kids, Ving said, "My dear guests! Go, the party is about to begin. . . ."

. . . For my serpents, who are very hungry . . .

Julie grinned. "I love strawberries!"

"And cookies are one of my essential food groups!" Neal added, nearly jumping up and down with glee. "I can't wait."

Ving smiled. "Then let my men take you . . ."

. . . To the room . . . the floor will give way. . . .

"I hope you find everything to your liking. . . ."

. . . Because no one will ever see you again!

Seven

Room of Tricks

The four children were led away from the giant chamber and into an arched hallway. Eric glanced around for ways to escape, but there were far too many bandits surrounding them.

"Parties are so cool!" said Neal. "Wait until Galen hears where we went! You hungry, Eric?"

"Um, not really," he replied, trying to grin.

Party! Eric knew they weren't going to any party. He just hoped there was a way to escape.

Icthos, the bandit with the broken wing, stopped at a door and inserted a large key. He threw aside the door and waved the children in.

"Right this way for food!" he said, with a clacking sound. Then Eric heard other words.

Food for the serpents — ha-ha!

The bandits pushed the children inside the room and shut the door quickly behind them.

"Okay, so . . . where's the food?" Neal asked.

It was a small chamber. The stone was as red as the rest of the palace, but stained dark. And it smelled damp, as if from water. All of a sudden Eric remembered what Ving had said.

The floor will give way!

"Climb the walls!" Eric yelled.

"Is that where the food is?" Julie asked.

"Do it — now!" said Eric.

The four children squeezed their fingers between the stones and pulled themselves up off the floor. Just in time.

Ka-foom! The floor split in two and fell away.

Splash! Beneath the floor was a pool of black water. The surface broke, and three scaly heads jumped out and snapped at the kids. *Snap!*

"Snakes!" yelled Neal. He kicked one away with his sneaker. "We're not going to *eat* the food. We *are* the food!"

"Now you get it!" said Eric, scrambling up the wall as high as he could go. "Ving tricked you!"

"But Eric, how did you know?" said Keeah, helping Julie climb up next to her.

"The tangfruit," he replied. "Ving tricked you with his weird magic voice. He makes himself sound good. But because I ate that fruit, I heard what he was really saying. And it was all bad."

They climbed halfway up the chamber walls. The serpents leaped up but couldn't reach them.

"Is there a way out of here?" asked Julie.

"Ask them," said Keeah, looking at Eric and pointing to a pair of green-furred mice nibbling crumbs on a row of stones near the ceiling. "Mice always know."

"Plus, the water's getting higher," said Neal.

The water *was* higher. It was splashing at their feet now, and the serpents were snapping again.

Snap! Snap!

Eric pulled himself up the wall. "Excuse

me, mice? I'm Eric Hinkle. These are my friends Keeah, Julie, and Neal. We were wondering —"

"Will you get to the point!" Neal cried.

Eric frowned. "Sorry. Okay, mice, can you tell us how to get out of this room?"

The green mice began to whisper in his ear.

"Uh-huh," said Eric. "Really? Wow. Sure. And then what? Oh. Uh-huh. Really? Okay, thanks."

The mice scampered away into the shadows.

"What did they say?" asked Keeah.

"Well, they've been here for a long time, so they know everything about the whole palace."

Neal nodded quickly. "Yeah, and?"

"And," said Eric glumly, "there's no way out."

"What!" cried Julie.

"No way out," Eric said. "We're doomed."

Neal nearly choked. "D-d-doomed? Oh, man! I'll never see Snorky again —"

"Or Max!" cried Keeah.

"Or Batamogi!" said Julie.

"Sorry," said Eric. "The mice said so —"

Pooomf!

Fireworks exploded in the small room.

Golden sparks showered over the kids and hissed when they hit the cold black water.

And then there was someone with them.

A man. A fairly young man. With a ponytail.

He stood clinging to the wall next to Keeah and Eric. He wore black boots, a long red cape, and a white scarf around his neck. He had a thin mustache and a short beard.

A shimmering, curved staff was slung in his belt. In his hand he held a short, glowing stick.

He grinned when he saw the kids. "Hi! Need some rescuing?" He pointed the glowing stick at the water. "Wand, send those serpents home!"

Zzzzz! A spray of sparks sizzled into the water. The serpents jumped and snapped once, then vanished into the depths below.

The black pool went still.

"That was awesome!" said Julie.

"That?" the man laughed a cheery laugh, tucking the wand in his belt. "It was nothing!"

"Wow, thanks, whoever you are," said Neal. "But, I mean, like . . . who *are* you?"

The man smiled. "People call me Shortbeard."

"*Short* . . . beard?" said Keeah, searching his face carefully. "You look a little familiar. . . ."

"But you can call me Galen," he added.

The princess gasped. "But it can't be!"

"But it is!" said the man. "Don't you like it?"

Eric's mouth dropped open. All at once, he, too, saw something familiar about the man.

They all saw it.

"Holy crow!" Julie said. "You *are* Galen! You were here when Tarkoom was destroyed four hundred years ago! And now you're here with us! So you're you! You're *young* Galen!"

The young man gave them all a quizzical look. "If you say so . . ."

Then, as quickly as they could, and all talking over one another, the four children explained how Tarkoom had appeared in modern-day Droon, how Galen was now four hundred years older, and why they had come to Tarkoom.

"If we don't stop Ving from changing Droon," said Keeah, "Tarkoom will stay. And Ving and his evil bandits will return to our time."

"You don't want that, believe me," said Galen. "But I just got here myself. I don't know what dastardly deed Ving is planning."

Eric frowned. "I heard him telling his bandits to prepare the bolt. Whatever that means."

Galen chewed his lip and shrugged at the same time. "Bolt, huh? Well, there are good bolts and bad bolts. There's a *bolt* of cloth. That's good. But I don't figure Ving is thinking about a change of clothes."

"Probably not," said Neal. "He's got all those feathers already."

"Right," said Galen. "Then there's a *bolt*

on a door. Could be that. Bolt also means to run fast. But that doesn't sound right, either. . . ."

Keeah and Julie gave each other a look.

"Plus, we have to rescue my dog," said Neal. "And Max and Batamogi, too."

"Ving sent them down below," said Eric.

"Then we need to split up!" said Galen, aiming his wand at the wall. He muttered a word and — *poomf!* — sparks shot everywhere. When the smoke cleared, there was a hole in the wall.

Galen bounded out to a high corridor.

"I'll head to the throne room. Ving is sure to be there," he said. Then he pointed down a shadowy hallway. "The stairs are that way. That's probably where they took your friends."

"I'll go," said Neal. "I hope Snorky is okay."

"I'll go with you," said Julie, smiling at Neal.

"Meet us in the throne room as soon as you can," said the young wizard. "We'll be teaching Ving not to mess with the good guys. And be careful!"

Julie and Neal snuck off into the darkness.

"We need to be careful, too," said Keeah. "We don't want to meet up with any bandits —"

"Ha! I eat bandits for breakfast!" Galen boomed. "Now, come on!" Then he grabbed Eric and Keeah by the hand and shot away down the hall.

Eight

The Bad Kind of Bolt!

The kids ran through the hallways, following Galen's flying cape and glowing wand.

"You're fast!" said Keeah, running to keep up.

"Not bad for a hundred and forty-two, eh?" Galen said, laughing. "Boy, I love this!"

Eric nearly laughed, too. It was funny to think that the old Galen they knew so well had been such a wild adventurer when he was young.

Suddenly, they heard clacking noises. They slowed down.

Before them stood the giant throne chamber.

Eric peered in. "The place is crawling with bandits," he said. "I don't see Ving, though."

But there was something else to see.

A round stone platform was rising up slowly through the floor.

On it stood something big and ugly.

A giant crossbow.

Eric had seen pictures of such things in history books. A bow was attached to a long, straight shaft. A thick cord was stretched far back and locked into place. But this had to be the biggest crossbow ever made. It was as big as a house.

And sitting on the shaft, poised and ready, was an arrow as long as a flagpole. At its tip was a jagged sliver of gold that spat and sizzled with what seemed like electricity.

"My gosh!" whispered Keeah. "I've never seen anything like that. It looks like a lightning bolt!"

"It is a lightning bolt," said Galen, his eyes darting around the room.

Eric slapped his head. "Of course! Lightning bolt! That's the kind of bolt Ving meant! And it's huge. But how will he steal treasure with that?"

"Let's not wait to find out," said Keeah.

When the crossbow was in place next to Ving's statue, six large bandits tugged on a large wheel at the base of the bow. The wheel turned.

As it did, the bow's shaft began to lift.

At the same time, the room's ceiling was gradually pulling apart to show the countryside around the Panjibarrh Valley.

"There is the Oobja village!" shouted one of the bandits. "Aim the bolt right at it! Hurry!"

Eric squinted to see, then his mouth dropped open. "It's Batamogi's village in the dust hills! They're going to fire this huge arrow at it!"

"There must be treasure buried under the mountain," young Galen whispered. "That's what Ving is after."

Keeah turned to them. "We can't let this happen. If that arrow destroys the poor village, it will change Droon forever!"

"It won't happen," Eric said, turning to the princess. "We won't let it."

Galen nodded quickly. "You bet we won't. I won't let these bandits escape into your world."

He pulled the curved staff from his belt. It was made of wood but glimmered with many colors as he swung it back and forth in the hallway.

"Cool," said Eric.

"My rainbow cutlass," said Galen. "I invented it myself. It'll make sure those bad guys never get a chance to use that bolt!"

Keeah glanced across the room. "Eric and I will take care of that big ugly crossbow."

"I like the way you think," said Galen. "All we need now is the element of surprise —"

"There they are!" snarled a bandit from inside the room. "By the door! Three of them!"

"Forget the surprise — let's go!" said Galen. With a single swift move, he jumped into the room, his cutlass whistling and sending off streamers of sparks.

The kids jumped in after him, running for the crossbow, but two bandits swept up into the air and swooped at them, their beaks clacking.

"No you don't!" Keeah said. She skidded to a stop and shot her hands out. "I'll stop you —"

Kkkk — blam! One red ball of sparks and one blue one blasted from her hands. They exploded together in a cloud of purple smoke!

The winged men fell to the floor, coughing.

"What was that?" said Eric, scrambling over to Keeah.

"Um . . . wizard *and* witch powers, I think," she said, blowing on her sparking fingertips. "It would be nice if I could control them!"

Fwing! Clang!

The wizard flicked his cutlass quickly and sent three more bandits spinning high into the air.

When they stopped spinning, they were too dizzy to fly. They fell to the floor — *thud-thud-thud!* — their eyes rolling around in their heads.

"Not so hawkeyed now, are you?" Galen said with a grin.

"YOU!" boomed a voice from behind them. "You will not laugh for long, wizard!"

The three friends whirled around.

It was Ving himself! He flew into the room, his black eyes blazing with anger. He thrust out his claws so fast they seemed to blur in the air.

"We don't need any tangfruit to understand you now, Ving!" said Keeah.

"Puny humans!" said Ving. "You will not stop me! My lightning bolt can destroy whole mountains. It shall destroy the Oobja village, too."

"The furry little guys make you mad or something?" Galen asked, whirling his glittering cutlass around in the air.

"Under their mountain is what I seek most!" Ving snarled. "The royal tombs of ancient Goll!"

The sly smile dropped from Galen's face. "But opening those tombs will release the old dark magic! You can't do that!"

"Watch me!" snarled Ving.

"No, you watch me!" Galen boomed. He whacked at Ving with his glittering cutlass.

Ving dodged the blow and lunged at the wizard with his claws outstretched. "Let the battle begin!"

Instantly, Galen and Ving pounced on each other, and — *clang-a-clang!* — the battle had begun!

Nine

Wild, Wild Droon!

Kwish! Fzz-ang! The large chamber echoed with the clashing of claw on cutlass as Ving and Galen fought.

In the confusion, five bandits jumped to the crossbow and began turning its heavy wheel.

Errck! Errck!

"The village is in our sights," Icthos called out.

"Fire when ready!" Ving shouted back as he lunged at Galen.

"Never!" cried Keeah. She shot a blue burst of light, and Icthos and the other bandits jumped away from the giant bow.

Eric ran with her across the room. They climbed up to the bow. "Let's aim it somewhere else," he said. "So Droon won't be changed."

"Good idea!" said Keeah. She and Eric gripped the wheel.

Kwish! Ving soared over Galen, flashing his claws at him from above. "Give up, wizard!"

"Keep your claws to yourself!" Galen replied. With a snap of his fingers, he soared to the top of the statue and landed on the giant stone head.

Glong! Clank! Across the statue's giant head, over the shoulders, down the arms, and back up again, the wizard and the bandit struggled.

"It's no good!" Eric cried, pulling on the heavy wheel with all his strength. "It won't budge!"

"Fire the bolt!" Ving shouted. Icthos scrabbled back to the bow. He began climbing up.

"Time for some special magic," said Keeah, her eyes taking on a strange look. Eric wasn't sure what it meant. Then she said, "Touch my hand. I think this will work. We can both turn that wheel."

"But it took five hawk men to move it!" Eric protested.

Keeah smiled at Eric. "We can do this. I'm sure we can. If I don't fry us both, I mean. . . ."

Eric blinked at his friend. Then he knew what she meant.

Keeah had begun to master her *other* powers.

When Eric touched her hand, he felt his arms tingle, first with cold, then with heat. Finally, he felt himself surge with strength. "Whoa! I feel really strong!"

Together, they gripped the giant wheel.

Errck! It began to turn. As it did, the shaft moved until it pointed nearly straight up.

"We're doing it!" Keeah said. "Keep turning."

"I'll stop you!" came a snarly voice.

It was Icthos! He had scrambled up behind Eric and Keeah. He reached for the firing lever.

"Fire the bolt!" Ving cried again.

"No!" Eric cried. He and Keeah turned the wheel once more as Ichtos pulled the lever.

Fwung — zwing! The bolt shot straight

up, like a long, flaming sword, right through the open ceiling and straight into the night sky.

"Yes!" cried Eric. "It's going off course! Batamogi's village is safe! Ving won't change Droon!"

Ving shrieked at the sight of the arrow flying harmlessly into space. He turned to the children.

"Bandits!" he howled. "Destroy them!"

"Not so fast!" came a yell from the hallway. It was Julie. She rushed in with Batamogi, Max, and Snorky. Three bandits swooped at them.

"I'll stop those nasties!" Max chittered. He spun a web of spider silk and flung it over the bandits' wings. They tumbled to the floor.

"And I'll finish the job!" Batamogi cried. He tossed a tangfruit at them and jumped away.

Crack! The hard shell broke on the floor, and the bandits ran out into the hall away from the smell.

From atop the statue, Ving trembled with rage. His black eyes narrowed at Keeah. "Old Goll *will* live again. And to make sure of it — I will destroy *you!*"

With one sudden move, Ving struck at Galen, then swooped at Keeah, his claws aimed like daggers.

"Keeah!" cried Eric. "Watch out —"

All of a sudden —

Poomf! Fireworks exploded in the room, light flashed, Ving was hurled to the floor, and a cloud of blue smoke covered everything.

A figure in a long blue cloak jumped from the smoke. He thrust both arms at Ving, his fingertips sizzling with sparks. It was old Galen!

"Begone, fiend, or you shall know what magic really is!" the old wizard boomed. "Goll shall remain in the past — and so shall you!"

Ving sputtered and snarled and clacked his beak in anger. But it was clear that Galen was ready to strike with all his might.

"You have not seen the last of me, old man!" the hawk bandit yowled. Then he picked himself up off the floor and jumped, and soared into the corridor after his bandits.

"Galen!" cried Keeah, hugging the old wizard.

"Hey, that's my name!" said the young Galen.

The old wizard turned to the young one. A smile crept over his lips.

"Well, well," he said. "Look at you!"

The two wizards studied each other closely.

Young Galen frowned and scratched his short beard. "Strange. You're actually me, aren't you?"

"Rather, you . . . are me!" said the old wizard, tugging on his long beard.

"This is weird and a half," mumbled Eric.

"You can double that," Julie added.

"I would," said Eric, "except there are too many doubles in this room already!"

Finally, the young wizard grinned a big grin and shook hands with his older self. "This is quite strange, even for Droon. But it's nice to meet you, old man!"

"Too bad we must leave now," old Galen said.

"Must we?" asked Keeah. "It's fun just

watching the two of you! The stories you could tell!"

"We must," old Galen said. "Because of that!" He pointed up through the open ceiling.

They could see that Ving's lightning bolt had flown straight up, blazing into the night sky, and was now starting to come back down again.

"It's heading right for Tarkoom," said Julie.

"Correction," said Max. "Right for the palace!"

"Right for where we're standing!" said Keeah.

"We'd better bolt!" young Galen cried. "Before that bolt blasts us! Come on, everybody!"

Eric started to run, then stopped. "Wait. Where's Neal?"

"Oh, dear!" said Max, trembling as he looked around. "We must have lost him in the halls. Poor Neal, I hope the bandits didn't catch him!"

Eric gasped. "We have to find him! We have to —"

Ka — boom!

The sizzling lightning bolt hit the palace.

It blew apart the giant statue of Ving and blasted a huge crater into the floor. Rocks and dust and flames exploded everywhere.

Suddenly, Snorky raced out of the chamber, barking and yelping just like he had that morning when Neal was chasing him. *"Woof! Woof!"*

"Snorky!" cried Eric. "Wait! Not you, too!"

But flames roared all around the room,

rising higher and higher. Smoke filled the air.

The earth trembled and quaked.

And the vast city of Tarkoom began to fall.

Ten

Friends, Friends, Friends!

Fwoosh! Boom! Flaming stones crashed down from the walls. Fire poured out through the hallways and corridors. The city of red stone turned into a city of red flame.

"We must leave before the city is destroyed!" said Galen, pulling everyone into a corner away from the fire. "We must go now!"

"We can't go without Neal!" cried Eric. Then, there he was.

Out of the smoke, Neal stumbled into the throne room. Snorky was nipping at his shoes to keep him moving. Everyone rushed to him.

Neal grinned as Snorky jumped into his arms and started licking his face. "He fetched me!" Neal said. "He actually fetched me! Finally, I have a real pet!"

"Excellent!" said the younger wizard. "Now we can all get out of here. Follow me!"

"No," the older Galen said. "We must go separate ways. You to the past, we to the present."

The young man looked at the older, and nodded slowly. "So . . . I guess this is good-bye?"

Old Galen smiled. "It is. But remember,

while your world has dark days now, they will pass. You must always believe in Droon. And love it."

"I will," his younger self replied firmly. "I mean, seeing you and these kids, I guess I always did believe. I mean, you did —"

"We both did, and do," said Galen Longbeard. "Now go to the storeroom. You will find a flying carpet. You must escape Tarkoom, or I would not be here. But be careful. There's danger."

The younger wizard grinned, his eyes twinkling in the light of the flames. "Danger? Old fellow, you just said the magic word!"

"You and your wild, wild ways!" old Galen said. "Now I know why my hair turned white!"

With that, Galen Shortbeard dashed recklessly across the burning room and into the hallway.

"He was so cool," said Neal. "I mean, *you* were cool, Galen. I mean, you still are —"

Just then — *eeeoow!* — a familiar howling echoed through the halls of the burning palace.

"Kem!" said Julie. "We forgot about him. He sounds mad that we busted up his city."

"We need to get out of here," said Eric. "And I know just the way. The passages!"

"Quickly, everyone," said Keeah. "Fast, fast!"

Eric led them all through the burning halls and corridors of the palace until he came to the garden.

"In the ground," Eric said. "Into the tunnels!"

They all piled into the hole he had fallen into earlier. Eric heard the furry mooples digging far away. He started for the sounds, worming his way through the dark passages.

Suddenly, Keeah tugged on Eric's sleeve. "Excuse me, Eric. This is the wrong way," she whispered. She looked at a tunnel on her left. "We need to go this way!"

"But . . . how do you know?" Eric asked.

Keeah blinked, then said, "I just know." She began climbing through the narrow tunnel. It turned upward. Soon they felt cool air wafting over them.

"I knew it," said Keeah softly.

Suddenly, Eric knew it, too.

Keeah had been in the passages before.

She was the lost little girl the mooples had told him about. She was the girl with nice manners.

Yes, it all made sense now.

It was in the passages, somewhere,

sometime, that Keeah and Witch Demither had met.

It was where Keeah got her witch powers.

Eric knew it, though he couldn't prove it.

And maybe it was in the passages — the passages that went everywhere — that Keeah somehow came to the Upper World. To his world.

Eric knew it all. He would find some way to tell Keeah. He would tell her. He had to. Soon.

"I see stars!" cried Batamogi. "Home! Home!"

They scrambled upward, and the cool air of the valley rushed over them.

Julie was the first one out, helping Max, Neal, and Snorky. Galen and Batamogi were next.

As his friends worked their way out of the passage and into the fresh night air of Droon, Eric paused.

He waited alone in the passage and listened.

He heard the voices of the friendly mooples cheering for them. He also heard sounds from everywhere the passages led to. He heard the washing of waves on a distant shore, the roar of flames, the singing of children in Jaffa City.

He heard the cry of the wind, of ice creaking in the frosty north, the hooting of birds in faraway forests, and the babbling languages of hundreds of different peoples and creatures from all across Droon.

"The everywhere passages," he said to himself. Then, as he climbed up through the hole and into the valley, he slipped onto his side.

And he hiccuped.

"Hic!"

And it all went silent.

The noises, the voices, the sounds.

All were gone.

The tangfruit's gift had worn off.

"Come on," said Keeah, taking him by the hand and pulling him up. "And look at .this!"

Behind them, the city of Tarkoom shimmered in the flames. The fire roared higher and higher.

Just then, Galen Shortbeard, perched on a small flying carpet, soared up over the smoke.

"He escaped!" said Max. "I like that boy!"

"He is unharmed, as are the bandits," old Galen said with a smile at his younger self. "They are just being sent back to their own time."

"And out of ours, thank you!" said Keeah.

As they watched, the scene before them shimmered once and faded. Young Galen vanished, and with him went Tarkoom, Ving, his hawk bandits, and the ancient past itself. The valley became still.

Once again, the honey-colored columns were tumbled and silent. The red walls were fallen.

And the great statue of Ving was no more than a mound of dust, blown smaller and smaller with each new breeze from the Panjibarrh hills.

Eeoow! The howling of Kem echoed across the night. It grew more and more distant.

"He got away!" said Eric, looking out over the purple valley. "Where do you think he'll go?"

Galen gazed into the west. "Probably to

find his first master. The one who created him."

"Who's that?" asked Julie.

"Ah!" the wizard said, still scanning the horizon. "You know him all too well. He is Lord Sparr."

Keeah gasped. They all did when they heard the sorcerer's name.

"I knew we hadn't seen the last of him," said Neal. "Even his name gives me the creeps!"

Suddenly, the air brightened behind them.

"The stairs have appeared," said Batamogi. "The Upper World calls the children back."

The small band of friends made their way over the silent plains to where the magical stairs stood shimmering on a hill.

"You have done good work today," Galen told Eric and his friends. "As always, we could not have done this without you. Now, Keeah, without delay, we must find Kem. Find Kem, and we shall find Lord Sparr!"

Keeah looked at Eric, Julie, and Neal. Then she shrugged. "Well, life in Droon is never dull!"

With a final wave to the kids, Galen, Keeah, Batamogi, and Max started across the plains and back to camp.

Eric turned to his friends. "Was that the coolest adventure ever?"

Neal grinned. "Absolutely. Until the next one!"

"We'd better get going," said Julie. "We have a kitchen to clean up. And a living room. And a dining room —"

"Thanks to Snorky," said Neal. He glanced around. "Oh, no, where's Snorky? Snorky!"

The dog came prancing over to the

stairs, licking his whiskers. His paws were stained with bright pink juice.

Eric gasped. "Uh-oh! Snorky ate a tangfruit!"

"It probably won't hurt him," said Julie.

Snorky licked his whiskers again. "Hurt me? It was delicious! But I want to go home now."

Neal's mouth dropped wide open. "Snorky . . . ?"

Snorky trotted up the magic staircase.

"Hmm," he said. "I wonder if humans can learn to fetch cookies. . . ."

The three friends stared at one another.

Then they all raced up the stairs for home.

ABOUT THE AUTHOR

Tony Abbott is the author of more than two dozen funny novels for young readers, including the popular *Danger Guys* books and *The Weird Zone* series. Since childhood he has been drawn to stories that challenge the imagination, and like Eric, Julie, and Neal, he often dreamed of finding doors that open to other worlds. Now that he is older — though not quite as old as Galen Longbeard — he believes he may have found some of those doors. They are called books. Tony Abbott was born in Ohio and now lives with his wife and two daughters in Connecticut.